The Life of a Coat

STORY BY **Kadya Molodowsky**

ILLUSTRATED BY **Batia Kolton**

FANTAGRAPHICS BOOKS

Our tale begins with a winter coat,
Not with a mischievous white goat.

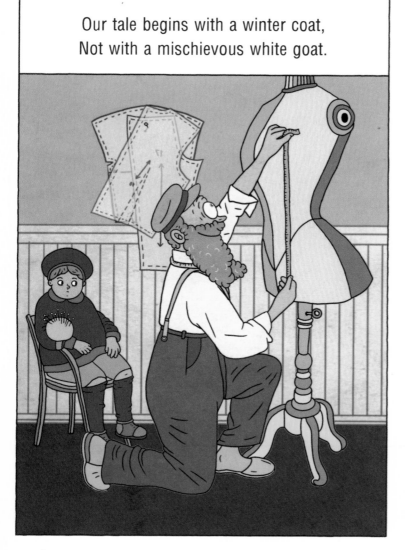

A winter coat with narrow slit
For a child's head to fit.

But oh, which child would it fit?
This winter coat with narrow slit.

Shmulik wore the coat with pride,
So he'd keep warm and snug outside.

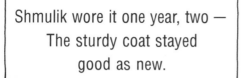

Shmulik wore it one year, two —
The sturdy coat stayed
good as new.

Another year — and yet, what's more,
The coat seemed nicer than before.

Little Shmulik grew and grew.
The coat grew tight. His flesh poked through.

Mama said (this didn't faze her),
Give it to Shmaryahu Lazer.

Lazer wore it one year, two —
The sturdy coat stayed good as new.

Another year — and yet, what's more,
The coat seemed nicer than before.

Until he raised his hands up high,
And both the sleeves tore. Lazer, why?

Bayla wore it one year, two —
The sturdy coat stayed good as new.

Another year —
and yet, what's more,

The coat seemed
nicer than before.

But one day,
Bayla bent down low...

Up, up —
watch the lining go!

Haya wore it one year, two —
The sturdy coat stayed good as new.

Another year — and yet, what's more,
The coat seemed nicer than before.

Oh the panic, oh the woe,
The girl is drenched from head to toe.

Crying hard, she couldn't stop it,
Haya lost the coat's two pockets.

15

Yechiel Peretz, wild and loud,
Donned the coat and
wore it proud.

Peretz, Peretz, what a clown,
Climbs a tree then falls right down.

Pulls the tails of mice and rats,
Plays his flute for dogs and cats.

Gets his father's goat with pranks,   Smiles through his mother's spanks.

Whistles, howls, and hoots with joy —
In brief, a rather happy boy.

Through it all,
this rowdy child
Wore the coat,
ran free and wild.

But that same day, at two p.m.,
He ripped the coat right at the hem.

And then at five p.m., you see,
He tore a hole above the knee.

Then at the closing of the day,
The collar somehow fell away.

Now the coat with holes was riddled,
In the bottom, top, and middle.

19

21

The poet KADYA MOLODOWSKY (1894–1975) was born in Poland.
She was a rambunctious, vivacious child who enjoyed writing poems
and aspired to be a teacher. Later, she realized her dream and taught
at Jewish preschools in Warsaw and Odessa. The children she met,
many of whom hailed from poor families, inspired her to write lively,
humorous poetry. She wrote in Yiddish, the language spoken by
these children. *The Life of a Coat* was written in 1931 to entertain her
students, some of whom didn't own a winter coat. Kadya Molodowsky
left Poland before World War II. She lived in Israel and the United
States, and continued writing in Yiddish all her life.

Translator: Ilana Kurshan
Editors: Conrad Groth, Rutu Modan, Yirmi Pinkus
Designer: Jacob Covey
Supervising Editor: Gary Groth
Production: Paul Baresh
Associate Publisher: Eric Reynolds
Publisher: Gary Groth

Fantagraphics Books, Inc.
7563 Lake City Way NE
Seattle, WA 98115

ISBN: 978-1-68396-267-0
First Fantagraphics Books edition: September 2019
Printed in Malaysia